THIS IS ME

THE ME I CHOOSE TO BE

Greatness Journey

EMPOWER YOUR CHILD

MINDSET STORIES AND SCRIPTS
TO EMPOWER YOUR CHILD

RYAN & JANUARY DONOVAN

DISCLAIMER. This is a work of fiction. Names, characters, places, and incidents are products of the author's imagination and are used fictitiously. Any resemblance to actual persons whether living or dead, businesses, events, or locales is coincidental.

We are not child psychologists or psychiatrists. Content provided is for self-development purposes and does not take the place of professional advice. Every effort has been made to ensure that all information included in this book is accurate and helpful to our readers at the time of publishing.

No liability is assumed for losses or damages resulting from the reader's personal application. You are accountable for your own actions and choices. Write to the publisher for specific questions regarding this disclaimer.

"Our self image, strongly held, essentially determines what we become."

~ Maxwell Maltz

Greatness Journey

EMPOWER YOUR CHILD

This book is dedicated to our children:
Jack Ryan, Pia, Ena, Bo, Ifa, and Vivi.
May you become a light to this world and
choose a life of Greatness.

AMDG

We thank God for his abundant love and mercy.

May our work lead souls to his divine adventure, and

may his light be the guiding path for all our children.

WE BELIEVE THAT THE ULTIMATE GREATNESS JOURNEY

IS THE JOURNEY WE TAKE TOWARDS THE DIVINE.

"The greatest discovery of my generation is that human beings can alter their lives by altering their attitudes of mind."
~ William James

"It's the repetition of affirmations that leads to belief. And once that belief becomes a deep conviction, things begin to happen."
~ Claude M. Bristol

ABOUT THE AUTHORS

Ryan & January

Ryan and January Donovan - entrepreneurs; podcast hosts; parents of six wonderful children; and creators of Greatness Journey, a mindset education company which provides helpful tools in empowering children to achieve their greatness.

Besides having a strong pulse in business, both husband and wife share a passion for contributing value to the world. Despite all the external influences that pose a threat to modern-day families, Ryan and January remain steadfast in raising their children intentionally so they'd grow with the same noble mission as their parents to create a positive impact and to gently touch the lives of others around them.

Ryan is a certified mindset trainer and coach, who has run several successful businesses. Meanwhile, January is a self-worth strategist with two decades of experience in training women on essential life skills. They have been married for 12 years now yet Ryan still enjoys to take his wife out on dates every Friday night.

Though they have already accomplished so much, both believe that they're still in the process of becoming the best version of themselves. They have always been relentless learners and dreamers and as their family grows, so do their goals and dreams.

CONTENTS

INTRODUCTION

The vision behind this SELF IMAGE STATEMENT Book is to help you design your child's Self Image before the world defines it for them. We have a self image crisis in our culture and if we are not deliberate about teaching our children how to see themselves, being worthy of good, then we risk having the world dictate how they should see themselves. Our goal is to help them see for themselves the best that they can be.

By intentionally putting these words into their conscious mind they can develop an awareness of the 'me' they choose to be. Their choice of words are powerful indicators of how they view themselves; their words will become flesh! Words are extremely powerful tools. This book will guide you to choose words that will EMPOWER and EQUIP your child to believe in themselves.

Through repetition these words will take root into the subconscious mind and form a habit. These habits are called paradigms. Paradigms are a multitude of habits that dictate our behaviors and cause our decisions. Cultivating your child's subconscious mindset to see themselves as strong, confident and valuable will build their resilience from negative influences.

We live in a culture that bombards our self worth, it is our duty as parents to be proactive about designing the image they hold of themselves. Through repetition, this book is designed to help shape your child's self image. Ultimately, their self image will largely determine how far they will go in life.

NOTE TO PARENTS

Cheers to awesome parents like you!

Fast forward 30 years from now. What tools would you wish you had given your children so they could build their dreams sooner? This may be a tough question to answer at this stage, but asking this question allows us to reflect on how we are proactively preparing our children to live great lives.

This is what '*Greatness Journey*' is about.
It's about equipping your child's toolbox with empowering tools that will help them maximize their full potential and become CONFIDENT in chasing their dreams.

But HOW do we prepare our children?

WE BEGIN WITH BUILDING THEIR FOUNDATION.
We train their mindset and equip them with the skill set they need to become resilient and self-confident.
We give them empowering words (called scripts) as foundational tools for their minds.

Words matter!
How they talk to themselves will determine the quality of their lives, so it truly does matter.

Write, Recite, Repeat!
Write: Rewriting scripts by hand is one of the most effective ways to program and retain new information. This stimulates a part of your brain known as the RAS (Reticular Activating System). The RAS acts as a filter for everything your brain needs to process. It literally helps you focus, and we know what you focus on expands. In *Write It Down, Make It Happen*, writing consultant Henriette Anne Klauser says, "Writing triggers the RAS, which in turn sends a signal to the cerebral cortex: Wake up! Pay attention! Don't miss this detail!"

Recite: Reciting the scripts as often as possible helps to ingrain a reflex response in situations. Reciting with emphasis and passion will get more emotion behind what you are saying. Emotion creates motion!

Repeat: By repeating the scripts through writing and reciting, you are implanting new words and thoughts into the subconscious mind. This will help you to memorize and, more importantly, internalize these scripts. When you repeat, you remember. This will help change paradigms and in turn increase confidence!

Training children to write, recite, and repeat these self image scripts will cultivate their resiliency skills and help build confidence.
These positive mental habits will become the lens through which they view the world.

Cheers to all our children!

Welcome to the Greatness Journey.

Onward and upward towards greatness,

Ryan & January

QUICK STORY

Jack, a 10-year-old boy, had been dreaming of an amazing treehouse ever since he could remember. He found the perfect tree in his backyard to build this dream. He saved up his money to buy all the materials for this epic tree house.

Finally, it was time to begin.
He opened his toolbox, and all he saw were three nails, an ax, and a broken hammer.

That's it…

Those were the only tools he had to build his dream.

Jack thought to himself, "How could I build a treehouse with only three nails, an ax, and a broken hammer?

Even if I wanted to, I wouldn't know how to with the tools I've got."

He quit before he even got started.

He quit because he didn't have enough tools in his toolbox.

Affirmations are tools... help your child fill their tool box.

HOW TO USE THIS BOOK

This is not your ordinary book. Its purpose is to develop your child's mental habits based on repetition. That means it's intended to be used often. Place this in a visible spot where you can ask your child to pick a script of the day or week. Ingrain it in their mind. Have them recite it to you often as part of their daily commitment. Make it fun: say it together with some emphasis and passion. Better yet, try singing it at times or even rap them like Ryan prefers to do with our children. Your task as a parent is to keep it fun, hold them accountable, and at the same time find real-life examples of how this applies to themselves or to others. Use your imagination and get creative to create your own family affirmations.

WHAT IS A SCRIPT?

A script is a guided phrase or sentence that helps to program your response in certain situations. Repetition of these scripts will impress them into the subconscious mind. Over time, your belief in them will strengthen, leading to a change in the way you think and, ultimately, in your behaviors. As your child writes, recites, and repeats these mental scripts, they will get ready to face challenges as they chase their dreams.

Step 1:
Read each page with the child. Engage them in a brief conversation about their thoughts. This will build awareness.

Step 2:
Encourage your child to work with one script per day or week.
Get your child familiar with the words and the
"Write, Recite, Repeat" process.

Step 3:
Put this in a visible location (night stand, coffee table, special chair).
Form the habit of letting your child work with one script at a time.

This Is Me

I can do anything I put my mind to.
I do my best always.
I persist until I succeed.
I take action right now.

I learn something new every day.
I grow from my mistakes.
It doesn't matter what anyone says,
I do what is right.
I trust my decisions.
I respect my body.
I honor myself.

I believe in my dreams.
I was born for a purpose.
I choose to laugh.
I choose peace.
I choose hope.

I choose to see what is beautiful
in this world.

I am worthy of love.
I am brave.
I am kind.
I am healthy.
I am fun.
I am free.

This Is Me:

(your name)

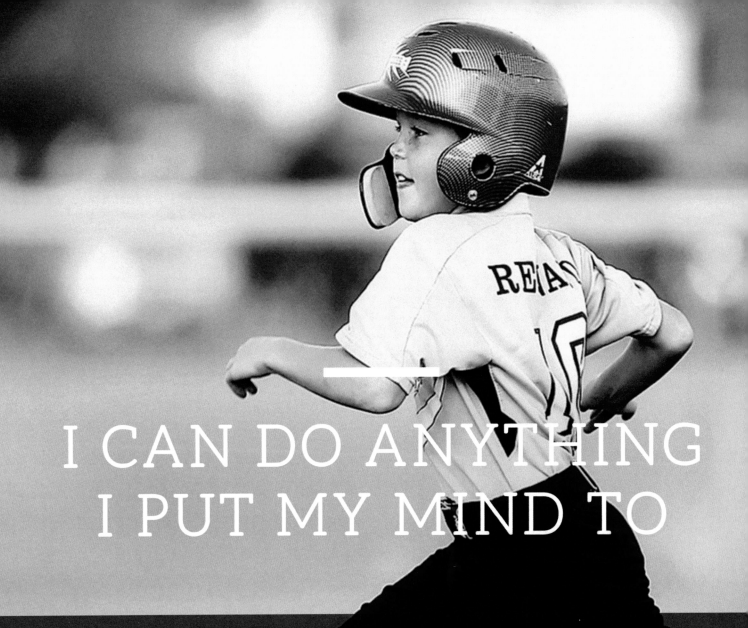

I CAN DO ANYTHING
I PUT MY MIND TO

I CAN DO ANYTHING I PUT MY MIND TO.
I practice hard. I am focused, and I give it everything
I have. I believe in my dreams, because I am confident
in my ability to do anything I put my mind to:
This is Me, the Me I choose to be.

STORY

Pia was getting ready to take her first-ever dive off the diving board. She had been working all summer to get enough courage to plunge head first into the water. She kept replaying in her mind what it would be like and how easy it was going to be, but she just could not get herself to do it. In her mind, she knew everything was going to be fine, but she couldn't quite take that leap. She had gotten close before... all the way to the very edge of the diving board, but the moment she would look down, she would scramble back to safety. She knew it was possible, though, because she saw all of her friends doing it. She knew that when she finally took that plunge, she would have the most fun summer, diving fearlessly over and over again with her friends. She knew she could do it; her fear was simply in her head. Pia had worked up the courage to start taking baby steps and start practicing her dives relentlessly from the pool steps and then the pool side. Finally the day had come for her to own her fear and take the dreaded leap from the diving board. It was late in the afternoon, and the sun was shining bright overhead. Her Dad saw her climb on that diving board, as though it was in slow motion, and he heard her say under her breath, five times: "I can do anything I put my mind to, I can do anything I put my mind to, I can do anything I put my mind to, I can do anything I put my mind to, I can do anything I put my mind to." Then Pia plunged into the water head first! Her Dad saw her rise from the water and say, "Daddy, I did it, I did it! I knew I could do it!" He looked at his daughter and thought, "Today, my daughter gave me a lesson on courage. I'm so grateful to be her Daddy."

EXPLANATION

There are going to be moments when you feel like you can't do what you want to do. You've tried, but it feels too hard. These are very important moments. These moments are special times in your life where you get to practice your strength and watch it grow.

This is your big chance to do something that doesn't feel so good, but you know it is good for you. So why do this? We know that growth only happens during these difficult moments. "No pain, no gain."

That's all it is: practice. You get to practice focusing your mind on something you want and give it everything you've got. When you feel stuck, recite your self-image script, and keep trying. You are going to surprise yourself. It will be exciting!

I DO MY BEST ALWAYS

I AM A HARD WORKER. I give one hundred percent of my energy to my work, and I stay focused. I am efficient with my time, and I am not afraid to be uncomfortable. I push past the discomfort and give it my best effort always. I focus on doing my best and not on comparing myself to others: This is Me, the Me I choose to be.

STORY

Joey worked so hard, but reading just did not come easily to him. "Why is it that my friends just seem to get it? Why does it take me forever to sound out the words?" He loved books, he loved words, but he was heartbroken because no matter how hard he tried, he could not seem to just read like everyone else in his class. He went to his Mama's room frustrated and said, "I'm just not a good reader, Mom, I quit". His Mom looked at him with a tender smile, sat him down so she could look him in the eye, and said, "I see a boy who works twice as hard to learn to read, I see a boy who is fighting to learn even though it feels hard, I see a boy who is not worried about what everyone else thinks, I see a boy who doesn't give up, I see in you, Joey, a boy who does his best regardless of how hard the task may be. I see your effort every step of the way, and that is what makes you a better you. I am not proud of you because of what you can do, I am proud of you because of who you are. I am proud of you because you fight to give it everything you've got, and I am confident that you will be reading in no time. Be kind to yourself, and know that I love you and that I see your work. That's what makes me the proudest." This gave Joey a new strength and determination. He wiped his tears, picked up his book with confidence, and started up his reading again.

EXPLANATION

What if you've tried your hardest to study for a test and, after all your hard work, you failed? It feels unfair. After you gave it everything you had, it seems that somehow your best was still not good enough. But who gets to decide what's "good enough?" You do.

Your grade does not reflect your effort. Your effort is the most important part. The purpose of learning is to bring out the best in you, regardless of the result. It's not just about memorizing. Doing your best in all you do is a simple habit of focusing all your attention to make your best effort: that's it.

Your best effort is good enough. Your best effort is not your best friend's best effort, your sibling's best effort, or your teammate's best effort. It is YOURS and yours alone. If you want to compete with someone, compete with yourself. Try to do better today than you did yesterday, and then a little better the next day, and the next, and the next.

I PERSIST UNTIL
I SUCCEED

I NEVER GIVE UP. I am resilient and I am persistent.
Hard moments just mean I need a little more practice.
I believe I am here for a special mission. I am not afraid
to persist until I succeed:
This is Me, the Me I choose to be.

STORY

Ally hated running. Every day during gym class, she would tell her teacher, "I quit. I quit and I quit." Ally knew that running would keep her body healthy - she knew it in her mind, but she had not built the habit of running, and her body was resisting. Her teacher, who saw Ally's effort in spite of her frustration, kept encouraging her as she ran: "You can do it, Ally, I believe in you!" Every day after she finished running her mile, she would look at her teacher and say, "I'm quitting running tomorrow. This was the last time. I'm not running ever again." Her teacher would simply smile and say, "I'm not quitting on you, Ally." A month passed, and her teacher no longer heard the grumble, the frustration. She no longer heard the words, "I quit." So she asked, "Ally, what happened? How come you've stopped complaining about running?" Ally looked at her with a smile and said, "Well, I just needed to build a new habit of running, and even though I hated it at first, I kept telling myself, "I persist until I succeed, I persist until I succeed, I persist until I succeed." Eventually a mile didn't seem so hard, so I just kept saying it, and now I forget that it was even hard. I actually kind of like it - well... I wouldn't go that far, but at least I don't hate it anymore. I am proud of me because I decided to persist and I succeeded."

EXPLANATION

Persisting feels like running five miles when all you want to do is quit, but then you decide to keep going step after step. Before you know it, you've run a total of ten miles! It's doing what you don't want to do when you don't want to do it so you can achieve a certain goal. Persistence is the key to achieving any dreams. It is a habit of keeping going, one step at a time, no matter how much you feel like quitting.

When you are in the middle of working towards your goal and all you want to do is quit, say to yourself over and over again, "I persist until I succeed." These words will help you go one small step at a time. Before you know it, you have already done it!

I PERSIST UNTIL I SUCCEED.

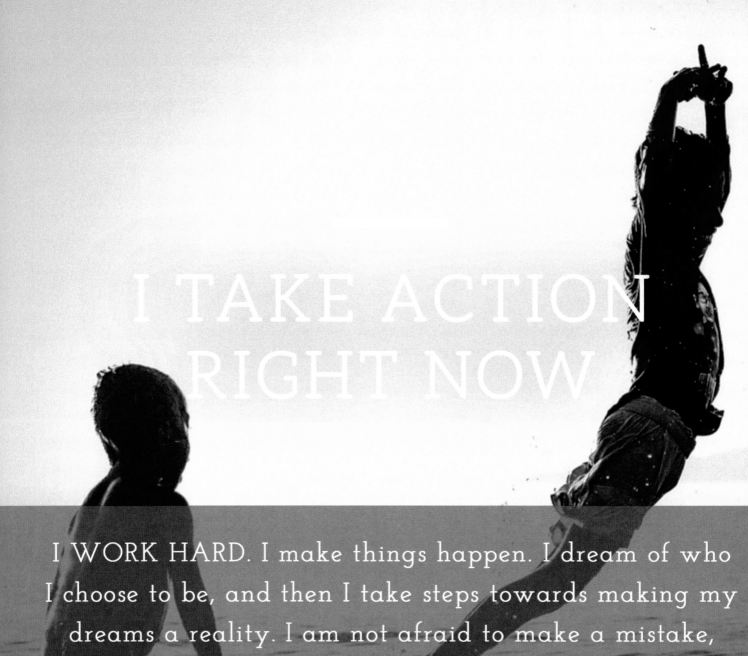

I TAKE ACTION
RIGHT NOW

I WORK HARD. I make things happen. I dream of who
I choose to be, and then I take steps towards making my
dreams a reality. I am not afraid to make a mistake,
so I am free to take action:
This is Me, the Me I choose to be.

STORY

Emma had chores she was responsible for, and every time her Mom would remind her to do them, she was quick to respond, "I will do it later, Mom." Her Mom finally sat her down and said, "Emma, if you don't take action NOW, you are going to miss opportunities that come your way because you are not ready, and you might regret it." Emma knew her Mom was right. She said, "Oh, thanks for the reminder, Mom. I better do my laundry so I can go on a playdate this afternoon." She went upstairs to grab her laundry and saw that it was a small mountain because she had put it off a few times. "Yikes!" She decided not to deal with it. "I'll do it later," she thought to herself. "Later" came at 3 pm. She heard a knock on the door. It was her friends Brigid, Colleen, and Sophia, all dressed in their swimsuits, ready to go the neighborhood water park. "Emma, do you want to go swimming with us?" they asked eagerly. Emma was so excited and grabbed her bathing suit so she could go ask her Mom if she could go. "Mom, can I go to the pool with Brigid, Colleen, and Sophia? The weather is perfect for it." Her Mom replied: "Sure, honey, as long as you are done with your laundry." Emma's heart sank. She didn't take action when she was supposed to, and now she was going to miss out on an afternoon at the pool. She was heartbroken, but she learned from it - she sat in front of the dryer all afternoon, waiting and hoping the clothes would dry before her friends were done at the pool. She told herself over and over again, "I take action now, I take action now, I take action now - never again will I have a pile of laundry..."

EXPLANATION

Taking action means you are moving one step forward towards something you want to accomplish. Why is this so important? Because your first step can sometimes be your hardest step. By waiting to do it later, you risk not doing it at all.

The habit of taking action, even if it's scary, will help you make brave decisions. Think of any dream, plan, or idea you have, and decide to take one small action towards making it happen. That step is going to lead to another step and, before you know it, you will have done it. You will look back and see that you have accomplished your goals; you will be one step closer to your dreams. Awesome!

I TAKE ACTION RIGHT NOW!

I LEARN SOMETHING NEW EVERY DAY

I LOVE LEARNING SOMETHING NEW EVERY DAY. There is always something exciting to discover. I am happy when I am learning, because it means I am growing. I learn something new every day and take action on it. The world fascinates me; it is a beautiful place to be. I choose to learn something new everyday: This is Me, the Me I choose to be.

STORY

"Bo, guess what, I'm taking you on a special adventure date!" Mom said. Bo answered excitedly, "Really, Mom!! Yay! What are we doing?" "Sushi, Bo - we are going on a special lunch date to learn about Japan." "Mom, but sushi is raw fish, and I'm only five years old". "Well, you can try the cooked option as a starter." Bo was pouting, "Mom, can't we just go get chicken?" "Oh, my darling, we are going to learn something new today. We are going to learn a whole new culture, and part of it is learning about their food." Bo responded, "Mom, but I don't like sushi." "How do you know you don't like sushi when you have not even tried it?" Bo said, "Okay, you're right about that." Bo walked into the restaurant, jumped onto the barstool, and watched the sushi getting rolled. He was fascinated. He had never seen it done before. He saw the rice, the vegetables, and how quickly the chef rolled all of it into perfectly shaped sushi. There it was in front of him: spicy tuna. "Oh, Bo, this is your moment to try something new! Take a bite." After seeing how the chef made the sushi, he had to try it and so he braved it. "Mom, I love it, it is so delicious... what is it?" Mom smiled and said, "Raw tuna! My son, you just learned something new about yourself today; you should be proud of yourself." Now, every time Bo goes on a special date with his Mom, he asks to go for sushi.

EXPLANATION

Do you know what makes a wise person? Wise people are like lamplights on the road. They light up the path so people can see where they are going. Imagine if there was no light. Then how could we see where we were going?

Now imagine if you were that person who would light up the path. You would get to guide other people in their journey. Wouldn't that be amazing?

So how do you become wise? Well, you can't learn it in school alone; you can't learn it in books alone. Becoming wise takes place through learning from all your many experiences. It is the application of what you learn and the experiences you gain from that action.

Every day, you decide to learn something new. It's like building those wisdom muscles. Before you know it, you are going to light up the world.

I GROW FROM MY MISTAKES

I AM QUICK TO LEARN FROM MY MISTAKES.
Everyone makes them. This is how I grow to be wiser.
I face my failures with gratitude, knowing I am braver
and better for it. They are a part of growing up,
so I am quick to move forward and learn from them:
This is Me, the Me I choose to be.

STORY

Wendi had a delightful collection of toy ponies. Her friend Nicole loved to play with them and secretly wished they were hers. One day, while Wendi was busy watching her favorite TV show, Nicole took a couple of ponies and brought them home without her Mom noticing. She hid them under her bed and only played with them under there too, just in case anyone saw her. Nicole finally got what she wanted, but it only made her feel unhappy. She didn't like feeling so secretive. One day, while she was playing beneath her bed, Mom walked into her room and asked what she was doing down there. Nicole took a deep breath and felt a big lump forming in her throat. But she chose to stop lying. She showed the toy ponies to Mom and explained how bad she felt about stealing them. Instead of getting angry, Mom helped her understand, "It's not always easy, but you have to do the brave thing." Nicole knew what she had to do. She returned the ponies to Wendi and said she was sorry for taking them. She is now happier and better because of her courageous decision to do the right thing.

EXPLANATION

Do you know anyone who has never made a mistake? Everyone makes them, whether they admit it or not. Yes, everyone!

But not everyone remembers to learn from their wrong choices. It's easy to feel sad when we've made a mistake, because we start to think that something is wrong with us. It's time to flip that thought.

Start thinking that there is really something wrong with you if you don't make mistakes. Failure is a key ingredient to success. If it doesn't happen to you, it could be that you're not trying hard enough. It makes you stronger; it means that you are trying something brave. You also need to celebrate these brave moments even when you feel like you've failed. Be kind to yourself. Decide to grow from your mistakes and to make better choices.

IT DOESN'T MATTER WHAT ANYONE SAYS; I DO WHAT IS RIGHT

I HAVE COURAGE. I push past my fears and do what I'm scared of anyway. I am strong. I am bold, and I believe I am on a special mission to uncover my greatness. I do what is right, regardless of what everyone else thinks, says, or does.
That's what makes me a strong leader:
This is Me, the Me I choose to be.

STORY

Tom lives near a marine sanctuary. It is a special place where fish and other ocean animals are protected. Tom's Dad works there, too. One afternoon, Tom saw a couple of boys throwing firecrackers into the ocean. They wanted to catch fish but were too lazy to do it the right way. Tom convinced the boys to stop what they were doing. If someone else saw them, they could be punished for breaking the law. The boys got angry. They warned Tom to never tell anyone or they would beat him up. As he walked home, Tom thought about what he should do. He knew that he should tell Dad, but he was scared the boys would hurt him or make fun of him. That night, Tom pushed past his fears and did the right thing. He told Dad about what he saw. "I will talk to the boys and their parents," his father said. "Don't worry, son. You only did what was right, and that is very brave. Look, I need you to be braver if the other boys are going to bully you. Be kind. Try to make friends with them." Tom felt upset. He didn't want to be friends with boys who hurt animals, but he understood why Dad suggested it. When he saw the boys at school, they threatened to beat him up. Again, Tom made the right choice. He smiled at them and said, "Dad and I are taking the boat out this weekend. If you want to go fishing, you can come with us." The two boys did not know how to answer. They were surprised that Tom was friendly to them. Finally, they agreed to go. Tom was happy about making the right choices. Inside, he felt more peaceful and stronger.

EXPLANATION

What if a bunch of your friends started making fun of the new kid in school? Would you join them, knowing it was hurtful? No, of course not. You would need to ignore what everyone else was saying in order to do what is right.

This is your practice toward becoming a great leader. Sometimes, leaders have to make unpopular choices to stand up for what is right. So don't doubt yourself.

Doing what is right requires you to be brave. This might feel scary, but you are going to see a braver "you" each time you have to stand up for what is right. That's what you call courage.

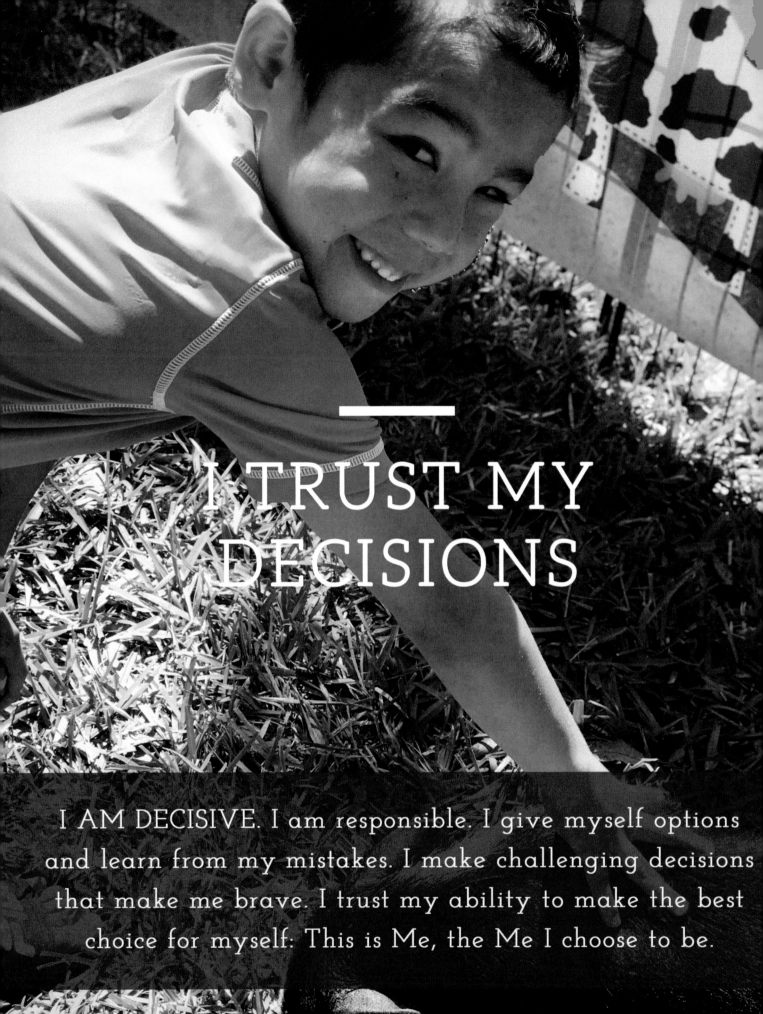

I TRUST MY DECISIONS

I AM DECISIVE. I am responsible. I give myself options and learn from my mistakes. I make challenging decisions that make me brave. I trust my ability to make the best choice for myself: This is Me, the Me I choose to be.

STORY

Cynthia loves to play with candles because they make her tea parties extra special. When she uses them, Mom or Dad always stand close by. They warn her that candles can cause dangerous fires, so they must make sure she is careful. One time, when her parents were busy cleaning the attic, Cynthia saw a bunch of candles in the kitchen. She thought what fun her tea party would be if she lit them up. She was confident that nothing bad would happen. Cynthia found a matchbox, then took the candles to her room. She was excited to use them, but she remembered what Mom and Dad told her. "Candles are not toys for children. Never play with them when we're not around, okay?" said her Mom. "Okay, Mom. I promise!" Cynthia felt bad about letting her parents down. They would be disappointed if she didn't keep her promise. It was hard to do, but Cynthia quietly returned the candles and went outside to play with her friends. She sacrificed her fun to make the best and most responsible choice. At that moment, she learned a valuable lesson. She discovered the true meaning of bravery; she made a firm decision.

EXPLANATION

Making a decision means you have to look at all your choices and then decide: which choice is going to make me the best me? Which one takes me a step closer to my goal, and which one takes me a step away from it?

People often get stuck at the point of making decisions, because they worry too much about failure. If you find yourself in this situation, just remind yourself that you won't always make the best choice and that it's just practice towards becoming a good decision maker. Trusting your decision is a very important skill for leadership, because leaders have to make a lot of difficult decisions. You have to trust yourself even when you know you might not make the best choice at that moment. Fail forward fast and learn from it. This is how you grow. When you feel doubt, read your self-image script and remind yourself of your own strength.

I RESPECT MY BODY

I RESPECT MYSELF. It is my responsibility to protect and to strengthen my body, because my body is a special gift. I take great care of it. I honor it because it is the only gift of its kind I will ever receive:

This is Me, the Me I choose to be.

STORY

Blake is different from most 8-year-olds. He eats his vegetables without complaining, then goes to bed early. This routine keeps him strong and healthy for sports. He is the baseball team's best player, and every day, he trains really hard for Little League. A day before the big game, Coach Keith told the team to rest. "Field's closed today, boys. Save all that energy for tomorrow. Eat your carbs, and get lots of sleep, because we'll show them who's a winner, all right?" Everyone cheered in agreement, including Blake. He went home early but ended up feeling bored, so he invited his younger brother to play some video games. They were in the middle of so much fun when Blake realized it was already 10 p.m.! "Please, just two more games?" his brother asked. "I'm sorry, Tom. It's past bedtime and my big game starts early tomorrow," he answered. "Okay." Tom shrugged and walked out of the room with a huge frown on his face. That night, Blake taught his brother a valuable lesson through his strong example. Even though Blake's team didn't win their game the following night, he felt like a true winner for respecting and taking care of his body.

EXPLANATION

Do you know that growing from being a child into an adult feels like going on a journey, kind of like being in a car? Your body is your special vehicle in this amazing adventure, which means that taking care of it is such an important part of growing up. When your body is well taken care of, you get to experience more of the beautiful world and the amazing people around you. You will have more energy to sharpen your focus and to help you work towards what you want to do and have in life. Remember, you only get one body in this life, so it is your duty to protect it, strengthen it, and keep it healthy. It's so precious, it deserves to be respected and cared for.

I HONOR MYSELF

I AM KIND AND GENTLE WITH MYSELF. I am patient with my mistakes, and I celebrate all the good in me. I am unique, irreplaceable. I honor who I am, because no one else will ever be like me in this world.
I am special: This is Me, the Me I choose to be.

STORY

Nate and Kelsie were the best of friends. They lived next door to each other and always played together. One morning, however, they got into a big fight. Nate called Kelsie some hurtful names and pushed her down. When she started crying because her knee hurt, he only made a silly face. Kelsie ran home and told Dad that Nate was mean to her. She was expecting that her father would help her by punishing the boy. To her surprise, Dad instead asked Kelsie to grab two pieces of bread from the fridge and spread strawberry jam on them. "Here, Dad." She handed the bread to her father. "That's not for me, darling. I want you to go out and give the other one to Nate." Kelsie was puzzled, but her father just smiled and told her, "Trust me. Being kind always works." She didn't feel so sure about it, but she did what Dad said. When she gave the bread to Nate, he was speechless for a few seconds, and then his face lit up. "Thank you," he said. They sat beneath a tree and enjoyed eating together. Because of one simple act of kindness, they became friends once more. Kelsie honored herself for being kind, even when she didn't want to.

EXPLANATION

You are on a very special journey called life. Here, you get to learn about yourself, about the big world, and about the many different people along the way. Your journey is unique. There is nobody else going through the same path, because no one else is like you. So honor yourself by celebrating your good days, and be patient with yourself in the hard moments. People will be unkind to you without realizing it, but stay gentle to yourself and to others through your words and actions.

I BELIEVE IN MY DREAMS

MY DREAM IS WORTHWHILE. I have a special dream in my heart that only I can fulfill, and it was given to me so I can share it with the world. I give myself full permission to aim for the impossible, even when it feels uncomfortable, because I believe in my dreams: This is Me, the Me I choose to be.

STORY

Becky watched her big sister Susan dance gracefully on stage. She moved so smoothly, the same way the ballerina inside Mom's music box did. Oh, how Becky dreamed of being a dancer too. Unfortunately, she could never be like her sister. She'd always break something each time she tried some ballet moves: if not her leg, then something else, like a vase or a glass lamp. "Dream on, Becky," she thought to herself. One day at school, the teacher asked the entire class to write about what they wanted to be when they grow older. Becky couldn't think of anything else. She only dreamed of becoming a ballerina, and so she wrote about it. By the end of their class, Becky was asked to stay behind. She wondered what the problem was. "Don't worry, Becky. You're not in trouble," said her teacher. "I just want you to know how talented you are. I've read your work, and I know how passionate you are about being a ballerina, but maybe you should consider being a writer." Becky's eyes widened. Her tummy felt like there was something warm and fuzzy inside. Those words made her realize that she had a unique talent. If Susan could dance well, Becky could make a masterpiece with her words. From then on, Becky worked on her new dream - writing a book of her own. She practiced writing stories. She read more books. Each day, she worked on improving her skill, because she believed in her dream.

EXPLANATION

What do you love? Who would you like to be? What would you like to accomplish, now or someday? The answer to these questions will lead you to your dreams, so don't be afraid to think of all the amazing things you want in life.

If you look around you, you'll learn that so many friendships, designs, inventions, and other accomplishments began in someone's dream. You have dreams in your heart that are special to you. No one else has the same. Your task is to keep believing and working towards your dreams even when it seems tough. It's only impossible until YOU can make it possible with hard work.

There are plenty of bumps along the road, but persisting through them will make you strong. Keep believing in your dreams. Don't give up, and never let anyone else convince you to give up. Your dreams are meant to come true, and they will lead you to something more beautiful than you've ever imagined. Say to yourself over and over again: I believe in my dreams.

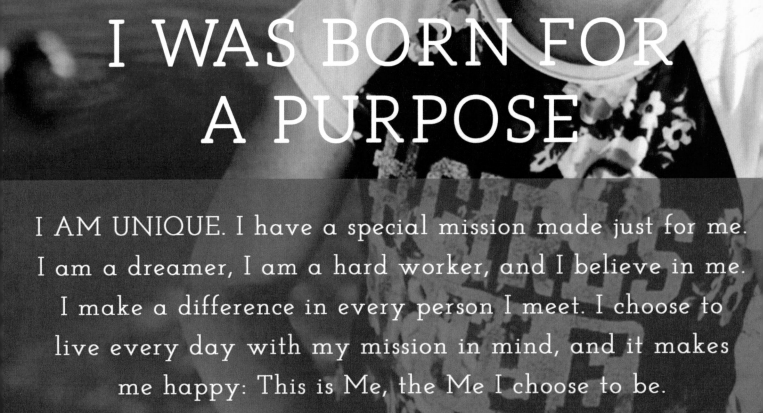

I WAS BORN FOR A PURPOSE

I AM UNIQUE. I have a special mission made just for me. I am a dreamer, I am a hard worker, and I believe in me. I make a difference in every person I meet. I choose to live every day with my mission in mind, and it makes me happy: This is Me, the Me I choose to be.

STORY

Patrick is a loving son who does simple things to make his family happy every day. He shares his room with his little brother Lance, who often gets terrible nightmares. When his brother wakes up shaking in fear, he rushes to Lance's bed and puts him back to sleep by telling him stories of brave superheroes. Sometimes, he will sing to comfort his brother. Patrick also enjoys setting up small surprises. Mom works as a nurse, so sometimes she stays in the hospital overnight. When that happens, Patrick cuts a piece of paper and shapes it into a heart. Then he writes a sweet message telling Mom how much he appreciates everything she does for him and Lance. "Thank you for being the best Mom ever. I love you!" Then, he leaves the message on Mom's pillow for her to find when she comes home the next morning. Patrick may not know it, but this is his special mission: to be a light in the lives of people he cares about. He chooses to spread love in his own family, and it creates a positive effect in their daily lives. Lance is learning to be courageous and loving just like his brother, and Mom always goes to sleep with a smile after reading Patrick's message. Through these simple gestures, he fulfills his unique purpose as an amazing brother and son.

EXPLANATION

Do you know that you are born with a unique mission that will serve this world and make it a better place? We call this purpose. Each person has something very special to give to the world that no one else can give except for them, because nobody else is like them.

How do you discover your purpose? Start by dreaming about the things you love, and then your dreams will change and grow with you. Allow yourself to dream of things that seem impossible! As you keep growing and working towards your dream, you will eventually be led to your purpose. You are going to change someone's world.

I CHOOSE TO LAUGH

I LOVE TO LAUGH. It makes my heart happy. I am a light, and I bring joy to the people around me. My joy is so contagious that people love to be around me. By spreading laughter, I make a difference in people's lives: This is Me, the Me I choose to be.

STORY

Holly and Jane were like sisters. At school, they sat beside each other and ate their snacks together. But one day, Holly was surprised that Jane didn't come to school. She asked their teacher about what happened to her friend. "Jane is very sick," said Mrs. Murphy. "She has to stay in bed for a long time." Holly was sad to hear the bad news. She would miss all the fun things she did with Jane. On the way home from school, Holly asked Mom if they could visit her friend. Her mother agreed, and they drove to Jane's house. When they arrived, they were greeted by Jane's Mom: "Thank you for coming, Holly. She has been missing you and school so much." Because Jane couldn't come down from her room, Holly went upstairs to see her friend. Jane looked really pale and sick, but Holly was just happy to see and talk to her again. She told Jane about what happened at school, and they laughed together. "Holly, we have to go. It's getting late," Mom called out. The two friends said goodbye and promised to see each other tomorrow. The next day, Holly visited and made her friend laugh once again. She cracked a few jokes and then told funny stories about their other classmates. What Holly did for Jane helped her to feel better. Instead of feeling weak and ill, she was always laughing because of her friend. She shared the gift of laughter, which may not cure a sick person but can touch hearts and light up the lives of those who are feeling down. It is truly one of the best gifts you can ever give away.

EXPLANATION

Who doesn't like laughing? There is something about it that makes all the worries and troubles go away. It's like medicine for the heart, which makes you much stronger. Laughter is also contagious; it brings people together. When you are around people who laugh, you want to laugh with them too.
So laughing is not only medicine for your heart but also for the people around you. It allows us not to get stuck in frustrating moments; it is a way for us to see past the hard moments and know things will get better. Laughing will make you see the world in a more positive way. It means that you are choosing to see the good, and in doing so, you bring light to the people around you.

I CHOOSE PEACE

I AM CALM. I am relaxed, I am patient. My worries don't take away my peace. Experience helps me grow wiser, and no matter what happens, I will choose to see the good. I am at peace, because it always gets better: This is Me, the Me I choose to be.

STORY

John's teacher asked him to arrange books into a neat pile. He was already halfway through when Bryce ran past the table where he was working and knocked everything over. This made him so angry. He was almost finished, but in a matter of seconds, all his hard work was gone. John ran after Bryce, but instead of starting a fight with him, John asked him if Mrs. Murray had also given him a chore to work on. Bryce nodded yes. He was actually in a hurry because the teacher had asked him to deliver an important note. John understood and explained what happened. He told Bryce that he felt bad about having to start all over again. Bryce apologized: "I'm really sorry, John. Here, let me help you out." The two boys had fun working together and became good friends. Because John chose peace, his patience gained him a new friend and more wisdom. He learned that punishing others is not always the right thing to do. Sometimes, a simple and honest conversation is enough to fix conflicts.

EXPLANATION

One of the most precious gifts that anyone could ever receive is peace. Peace means that you are free to be your own unique self while growing to become a better version of you. Both of these ingredients are needed to find peace..

Peace is so important that, without it, we can't appreciate all the gifts that we have been given. We become tired and frustrated. Peace also allows us to hope. It is so precious that it needs to be protected. That means that you have to find ways to keep your heart calm and relaxed.

Peace does not mean that you don't have worries. It means that you can teach yourself to remain calm even in hard moments, because you believe that things will get better. Be at peace; be a gift to the people around you.

I CHOOSE HOPE

I BELIEVE IN PEOPLE. I believe in myself. The world is a beautiful place filled with amazing people. There is so much good and beauty around me. Every day, I am excited to see what comes my way. I am filled with hope, and I share it with those who need it in their lives: This is Me, the Me I choose to be.

STORY

Everyone in Cathy's family loved to sing. Her sisters were members of the glee club and were really entertaining performers. Cathy enjoyed watching them each time they had a show. Cathy was different, though. Unlike her sisters, she was too shy to perform on stage. "I don't sing as well as they do," she told people when they invited her to try. She hid her talent from the world. Then one day, one of her big sisters talked to her. Bella wanted her to join them for a fundraising concert, where people would pay for tickets and their money would go to helping poor people. Cathy wanted to help out so badly, but she didn't feel confident enough. "You'll never break out of that shell unless you try," her sister said. "Just try singing with us, this one time. You have a beautiful talent, Cathy. Share it. Use it to serve those in need." Cathy thought hard about what her sister said. Every word of it was right. She could sing well, too. If she joined her sisters, the show would surely be more enjoyable too. "Okay, I'll do it!" She took that one big leap, and that changed her life for the better. She became a better singer, and more importantly, she became more confident about herself. Cathy decided to believe in herself that one time, but that moment was all it took for her to grow. Just one little seed of hope, and look at where she is now: she sings in front of crowds. She shares her talent, and she's no longer afraid.

EXPLANATION

Hope is believing that things will always get better. It means that you are never giving up, because you know there is always something better coming your way. Hope requires you to imagine all the beautiful things that are about to happen. It means that you see so much good in people and the world that you can't help but get excited about the future. Without hope, the world would be a sad place; no one would ever be happy. When you hope in people, you help them grow into a better version of themselves. That is one of the most beautiful gifts you can ever give, so keep believing and keep hoping that life will always keep getting better. Move onward and upward towards a more beautiful life.

I CHOOSE TO SEE WHAT IS BEAUTIFUL IN THIS WORLD

I AM POSITIVE. I live in a world that is peaceful, beautiful, and filled with amazing people. I am surrounded with so much good. I am full of hope, and I choose to see what is beautiful in this world: This is Me, the Me I choose to be.

STORY

"Hurry, Mom, Dad! We might miss the sunrise." James pulled his parents' arms as he ran towards the end of the park to catch a breathtaking scene. This had been an annual tradition of their family, and as James was enjoying his meal, he couldn't help but notice an old man dressed in torn and dirty clothes glimpse at them from a short distance. James felt uncomfortable and asked, "Mom, isn't it impolite to stare at people, especially when they are eating?" His Mom threw a question back at him, "But James, isn't it impolite and inconsiderate for us to be having all the fun we could get while there are people who couldn't even have a decent meal?" James was speechless for a moment. His Dad gave him a gentle look and said, "You know, son, we live in an imperfect world. It's hard to identify the people who make good choices from the ones who make poor ones, but we need to understand and love each and every one." He explained the importance of always finding the positive side of a person so that we may live in harmony. Upon hearing those powerful words from his parents, James stood up and went straight to the man who was looking at them. He said, "Hi, kind Sir, I noticed you from our picnic area and would like to invite you over for some sandwiches and juice." The man was hesitant, but James' parents stood smiling while waving at the two. They had the most unforgettable sunrise experience as a family and even gained a new friend. From then on, James has chosen to become more aware of the people around him, for he learned the valuable lesson of showing care to everyone despite their differences. Now, he sees the world as an opportunity to extend the love he has been getting from his own family.

EXPLANATION

In every situation, you have a choice to see either the good or the bad. That choice will determine how you see the world. Even the bad moments can have so much good to offer if we decide to learn from them. By searching for what you can learn from every situation; you will be able to see how beautiful this world truly is. It all depends on one thing: your choice.

Choosing to see the good will bring so much peace in your heart and in the hearts of many other people. Your decision to see what is good and beautiful in the world will encourage everyone around you. You will bring hope to so many people's hearts. Each time you are in a tough situation, tell yourself, "I choose to see what is beautiful and good in this world," and you will find it.

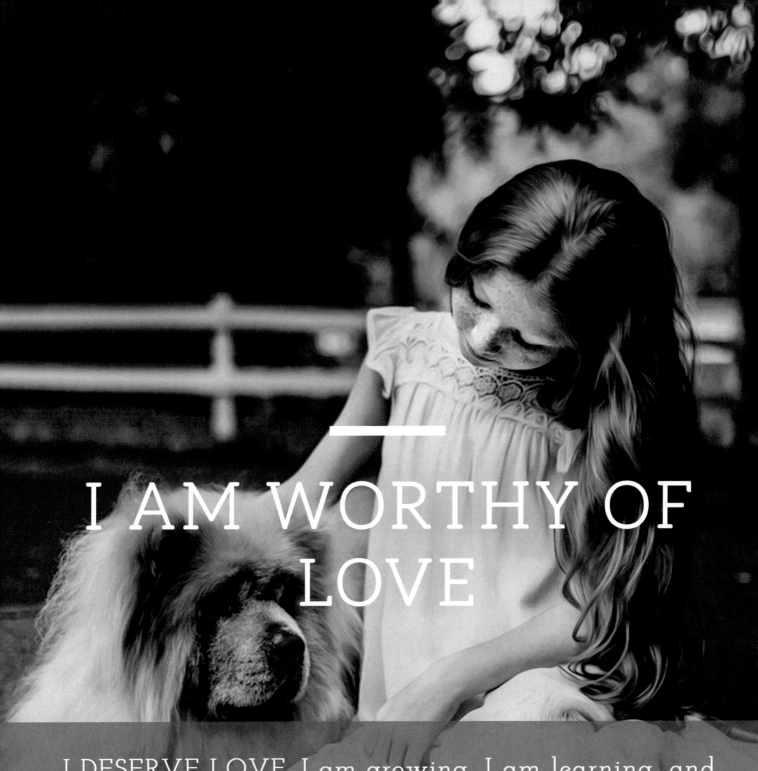

I AM WORTHY OF LOVE

I DESERVE LOVE. I am growing, I am learning, and
I am becoming better every single day. I believe
I am good, and I am whole, in spite of my mistakes.
I respect myself because I am worthy of love:
This is Me, the Me I choose to be.

STORY

Ben was not going to put up with Timothy's rudeness anymore. Timothy said he was Ben's friend, but he would always make fun of what Ben was wearing or the way Ben talked and walked. Ben didn't like the way Timothy made him feel, but he lived down the street, so he felt like he had to play with him; he was his friend. One day, Ben came in crying to his Daddy, who asked, "What's the matter, Ben?" Ben said, "Timothy is mean, Daddy. He says he is my friend, but he always makes fun of how I talk, and I don't like it." His Dad put little Ben on his lap and asked, "Why do you continue to play with Timothy?" Ben replied, "Because he is my friend. "Dad asked, "Should friends treat you unkindly?" "No." Ben said. "You're right, Ben. Friends should not treat you unkindly; that's not a friend. "Ben's dad looked him in the eye and said, "listen, I am proud of you for being a good friend, for playing with Timothy, because not a lot of children in the neighborhood want to play with him. I am proud of you for being kind even when he is unkind. However, I am going to remind you that you deserve to be treated kindly. You are worthy of love. You must not allow people to treat you unkindly, and it is OK not to be his friend. Can I give you a script to talk to him, the next time he makes fun of you?" Ben responded, "OK, Daddy." "You can say, 'Timothy, friends don't treat each other rudely, and if you continue to make fun of me I will no longer be your friend. I deserve to be respected.' If he continues to do it, you need to tell me, and then we need to stop hanging out with him. Ben, I want you to know that you don't have to allow people to treat you rudely. You can walk away and find new friends. There are a lot of people who want to be a friend to a kind person like you, so don't waste your time with people who do not respect you. You are worthy of kindness and love, my son." Ben looked up at his Dad. "So it's OK if I am no longer his friend?" "It is more than OK, my son." Ben knew his Daddy was there to protect him, so he decided to tell Timothy that he needed a friend that was kinder. It wasn't long until Ben met Andrew, another boy down the street, who was kind and so much fun.

EXPLANATION

You are loved, you are respected, and you are worthy of all the beautiful things in this world. Just by being here, you have already changed the world.

Being worthy of love means that you deserve to receive it, no matter what you have done. Your mistakes do not determine whether you are lovable or not; you deserve love regardless of how you feel about your mistakes. Every person is worthy of love. It is a gift that everyone deserves, including you. You deserve for people to take care of you and make you feel special because you MATTER, what you think matters, your dreams matter. and your life matters. Whatever comes your way, remind yourself that you are worthy to be loved. when you challenge people sometimes they rise to the challenge and other times they choose not to. Both the art of challenging and the strength to not settle are important of being worthy.

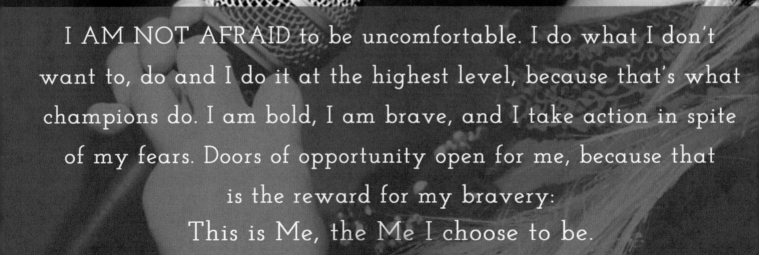

I AM BRAVE

I AM NOT AFRAID to be uncomfortable. I do what I don't want to, do and I do it at the highest level, because that's what champions do. I am bold, I am brave, and I take action in spite of my fears. Doors of opportunity open for me, because that is the reward for my bravery:
This is Me, the Me I choose to be.

STORY

Jimmy was an average middle school student. Like many, he liked baseball and video games. He was a good friend to everybody, and his parents taught him to be kind. One normal school day, right after the bell rang for dismissal, he ran across a group of kids who were forcibly taking another student's wallet. He didn't want to interfere, as he might get sent to detention along with them. Jimmy walked faster without looking back. When he got home, he shared this with his Mom and said how he felt bad for the kid who was getting bullied. Jimmy's Mom paused for a while and said, "Honey, I know it's not nice to meddle with other people's business, but if it is already causing harm and injustice, there is a need to speak up or at least do something about it." Jimmy said he was afraid of being associated with the bullies and ending up getting punished for something he wasn't guilty of. His mother countered this by saying, "The truth will make you a better person, no matter how hard it is to stand up for what you believe is right. You have to be brave enough to do it. That's the only time you will grow." That night, there was a debate going on in Jimmy's head. At one point, he knew that those kids might hurt him as well if he chose to expose their wrongdoings. But he was reminded of his mother's words of wisdom. The next day, Jimmy walked slowly into the principal's office and retold the unfortunate incident. He was willing to testify against the bullies so that it wouldn't have to happen to anyone again. The principal agreed and thanked him for his bravery and courage to step up for what is right.

EXPLANATION

Being brave feels like singing on stage in front of thousands of people for the first time. You want to do it, but at the same time you are afraid, because it's a scary feeling. Even when every part of you is saying no, you choose to do it anyway. That is your moment of courage. You know deep in your heart that you have just conquered something huge, and you have become a braver person for it.

As you grow older, you are going to have more opportunities to be brave. In many situations, you will be asked do something you don't feel like doing, but you will choose to do it anyway because you know it will be good for you. The more courageous steps you take, the more doors of opportunity you will find open. That is your reward for being brave. Feeling afraid is normal. Everyone experiences it. How we respond to it is what makes all the difference. Find those uncomfortable moments throughout your day where you can practice being brave and remind yourself that this is you: You are brave.

I AM KIND

I AM KIND. I am patient. I am thoughtful. I am tender with myself. I respect who I am, and I respect others, even if I don't agree with them. I am quick to find ways to make people feel important:
This is Me, the Me I choose to be.

STORY

Annie excels in her academics. In fact, she wants to become a doctor someday. Every night, she spends at least two hours reviewing and reading books to maintain her straight A's in school, not only to make her parents proud, but also to make a good start to her promising journey. However, everything changed when she had a new brother who would scream and cry all day long, especially at night. It became harder and harder for Annie to focus on her lessons as she constantly got distracted. One night, she couldn't take it anymore, so she approached her Mom and ranted about how her newborn brother was disturbing her study habits. Her mom sat her down while holding the baby in one arm. "Annie, you are so precious to us, we want you to grow up smart and diligent, but that's not all. You also have to know how to help others shine and let them build up their own confidence. It's by simply being compassionate, loving, and kind." Annie felt a little ashamed, "Mom, I know I have disappointed you and hurt your feelings. How can I make it up to you?" Her mother smiled and said, "How about we schedule date nights in a quiet coffee shop so you can read a book peacefully, or set sleepovers with your cousins once in a while so you can take a break?" "Sounds fun!" Annie exclaimed. Annie realized that there is a need to adjust and make arrangements to make everything work for everyone's benefit. She also acknowledged the fact that now that she's a big sister, she has responsibilities not only for herself, but to her baby brother, which requires more patience and kindness.

EXPLANATION

Kindness allows us to think about how people feel, what they might need, and how we can help them. It shows people you care about them and appreciate them. Kindness is being patient when someone makes a mistake. It is encouraging others when they feel sad and finding small ways to make people feel special. Kindness is how we talk, how we act, how we treat people around us, and how we treat ourselves. Being gentle and patient to ourselves is so important because unless we begin practicing kindness, we can't be kind to the people around us. That's how it works. Kindness brings peace to our hearts and to other people's hearts. It is what makes this world a more beautiful place.

I AM HEALTHY

I AM HEALTHY. I am strong. I am responsible for my body. I take great care of myself. I choose healthy food, I drink lots of water, I get enough rest, and I love to exercise. I protect my mind from negativity because I choose to have only happy and healthy thoughts: This is Me, the Me I choose to be.

STORY

Dan and Marty are brothers who love to eat sweets. They can finish an entire bag of candies in minutes but they both don't know how to take good care of their teeth. They would go to bed without brushing their teeth, which is why Mom made a strict rule that they can only eat a couple of sweets every week. Dan, being the older one, was responsible even when there weren't people around. He disciplined himself by going over what damage his teeth could suffer if he continued his unhealthy habits. Marty, on the other hand, still bought bags of sweets and ate them when his brother wasn't around.

He thought he could get away with it until one day, his teeth started to hurt. The pain was still tolerable at first but soon enough, he was already crying for help, "Mom, please take me to the dentist!"

Their mother was so surprised when Dr. Fitz told her that Marty's teeth have been badly damaged by sugary treats. Marty felt bad about his dishonesty and realized that he made a big mistake. Besides breaking his family's trust, it would take awhile for the dentist to fix his teeth. He could only apologize to Mom and his brother, then promise he won't lie or sneak up on them again.

EXPLANATION

Being healthy is a choice to be responsible for the gift of your body. It is keeping your body free from junk and toxins because it deserves to be taken care of. The more you take care of your body, the stronger and more resilient you become, which means that you will have plenty of energy for adventures. Being healthy also means getting enough hours of rest a day; it means drinking at least ten glasses of water a day; it means eating lots of fresh food, especially fruits and vegetables. It also means moving and exercising so you can keep your body strong for the many exciting adventures coming your way. It means taking great care of your mind, because your mind helps you take care of your body.

I AM FUN

I AM FUN, I am free, I am happy.
I choose to see what is good and beautiful in my world.
I bring joy, I bring light:
This is Me, the Me I choose to be.

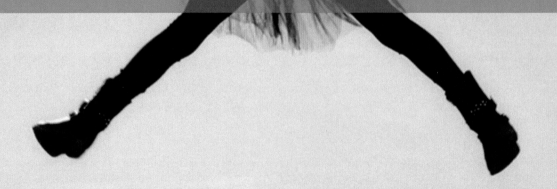

STORY

Kristie had a new set of crayons and was using them to make a colorful drawing of their house, when her three-year-old brother Andrew just popped up beside her. He could barely talk, but he pointed at the crayons with an excited smile on his face. "I draw train, too." However, Kristie didn't want to share. Her little brother didn't even know how to hold them properly. She was afraid that he might break them or eat them! "No, Andrew. These are not for babies." He responded with a very sad look on his face. Kristie felt sorry for her brother, so she just gave him a couple of colors she didn't like. When Andrew began working on his train, she realized that he enjoyed drawing so much. She checked her box of crayons and thought that there were enough colors for both of them to share. Her brother picked blue, which was his favorite color, and drew happily on his paper. When Kristie offered to help him make a blue truck, Andrew's smile widened. He nodded yes and then spent the entire afternoon having fun with his big sister. Through the simple act of sharing, Kristie lightened up Andrew's day. Her decision made her feel good about herself and it made her feel free, knowing that she didn't hurt other people.

EXPLANATION

It's hard to describe what fun is, but it's easy to know when you're in it. It brings this happy feeling that makes you want to stay in it. Take note: there is a big difference between making fun of someone and having fun with someone. Making fun is unkind and hurtful, and it takes away something from others, while having fun is sharing a special, sweet time together. It is sharing something that brightens your day; it is choosing to see what is positive, the good and the beautiful.

I AM FREE

I AM FREE, I am happy, and I love being my best me.
I am free to try something that is beyond me, because
I am quick to learn from my mistakes. No one else will
ever be like me. I am free to become the best I can be,
because I love being me:
This is Me, the Me I choose to be.

STORY

Anne had a really tough time reading when she was younger. According to the doctor, she was suffering with a learning disability called "dyslexia." When she looked inside books, it seemed that letters on their pages moved around or exchanged places with each other. It was also hard for her to read out loud, too. She read too slowly for someone her age, and she often mentioned words that weren't even there. This is why she felt so scared as soon as the teacher asked her to read a short poem to the entire class. "I'm sorry! I need to use the bathroom!" Anne jumped up from her chair and ran inside one of the bathroom's cubicles. She locked the door and began crying. She stopped when someone called her name a few minutes later. It was her teacher, Mrs. Dudley. "Anne, are you there? Please tell me what's wrong." Anne was silent at first. She was too embarrassed to admit the truth. With whatever courage she had left inside of her, she confessed, "I don't know how to read!" Her teacher leaned closer to the door of her cubicle. "Your Mom told me about it. Don't worry, your classmates and I will help you out. Trust me." Luckily, Anne believed in Mrs. Dudley and returned to the classroom. Her fingers were shaking as she tried to open the book. She was so terrified that her seatmate Jerry got up from his chair to help her out. Anne hesitated, but when she looked around the classroom, everyone was wearing a kind smile on their faces. She began to read very slowly, and she got stuck every time she made a mistake. When that happened, Jerry whispered the right word into her ear. Her other classmates helped, too. No one ever laughed at her disability. Instead, they made her feel accepted and supported. Before she knew it, Anne had already finished reading a couple of paragraphs. That day, she won over her dyslexia. Through the help of her teacher and classmates, she fearlessly opened her true self to other people. She grew into a braver and better version of herself.

EXPLANATION

Do you know that there are no two people alike? That means that there is no one like you in this world, and nobody will ever be you. Who you are and what you choose to do is going to be so important. No one else can do what you do. Your actions will affect the lives of the people around you. This is a big responsibility and, at the same time, an opportunity.

Being free to be you means that you love yourself and the many different parts of you that make you irreplaceable, even those parts about you that you are not crazy about. Being free to be you doesn't mean you stop trying to be the best you. It means that while you are trying your hardest to become the best version of yourself, you are free to make mistakes, learn from your falls, and keep on trying. When you are free to be you, then you are not afraid to try something new; that is how you grow.

THIS IS ME

Greatness Journey

EMPOWER YOUR CHILD

CLOSING THOUGHTS

You have the power to choose to become your BEST YOU.
You are responsible.
You are beautiful, and you are good.
Who you become is a choice and a privilege.

At every moment, you can learn to become
the best that you can be.
You are free to grow, you are free to fall, you are free to learn,
you are free to choose whoever you want to be.

You have a purpose, you have a choice, and
both matter to the world, because the world needs you.

The world needs your light.
The world needs your voice.
The world needs you to make a WISE choice.

You can choose who you want to be; that's what makes you free.
You can create something meaningful, something remarkable.
You can dream of the impossible and work hard toward your
highest goal.

You can design the world you choose.

You can choose hope.
You can choose love.
You can choose peace.
You can choose to see what is good in this world.

You are free to respond; that is a choice.
You are free to choose the YOU you want to be.

You get to DECIDE the YOU you want to be.
This is you!

Greatness Journey
EMPOWER YOUR CHILD

Donovan Creed

I can do anything I put my *Mind* to

I can do all things through *Christ* who strengthens me

I do my *Best* always

I learn something new *Everyday*

I take action right *Now*

I *Persist* until I succeed

It doesn't matter what anyone says – I do what's *Right*

I'm not afraid *Jesus* is with me every where I go

I can, I will, I must – be a *Saint*

*J*ESUS I TRUST IN YOU

May your children be the light that the world needs now.

Cheers from our family to yours,

The Donovans

Made in the USA
Middletown, DE
10 December 2022

17979179R00035